Hygiene...
YOU STINK!

"For all the little stinky forks out there, this one's for you!"
~ Julia

Stay
CLEAN
like
Jean!

Written by
JULIA COOK

Illustrated by
ANITA DUFALLA

'JAKE' 'ANGUS' 'KIRBY'

BOYS TOWN
Press

Boys Town, Nebraska

D1294693

Hygiene... You Stink!
Text and Illustrations Copyright © 2014 by Father Flanagan's Boys' Home
978-1-934490-62-4

Published by the Boys Town Press
14100 Crawford St.
Boys Town, NE 68010

For a Boys Town Press catalog, call **1-800-282-6657**
or visit our website: **BoysTownPress.org**

Publisher's Cataloging-in-Publication Data

Cook, Julia, 1964-

Hygiene... you stink! / written by Julia Cook ; illustrated by Anita DuFalla. -- Boys Town, NE : Boys Town Press, c2014.

p. ; cm.
ISBN: 978-1-934490-62-4

Audience: K-6th grade.

Summary: Jean-- a stinky fork in the silverware family-- hates taking a bath in the sink and detests showering in the dishwasher. In this clever tale, young readers are sure to get the message that good hygiene will improve their health and their relationships!--Publisher.

1. Children--Health and hygiene--Juvenile fiction. 2. Hygiene--Juvenile fiction. 3. Baths--Juvenile fiction. 4. Health--Juvenile fiction. 5. Interpersonal relations in children--Juvenile fiction. 6. Children--Life skills guides. 7. [Children--Health and hygiene--Fiction. 8. Hygiene--Fiction. 9. Baths--Fiction. 10. Health--Fiction. 11. Interpersonal relations--Fiction. 12. Behavior--Fiction. 13. Conduct of life.] I. DuFalla, Anita. II. Title.

PZ7.C76984 H94 2014

[E]--dc23   1408

Printed in the United States
10 9 8 7 6 5 4 3 2 1

Boys Town Press is the publishing division of Boys Town, a national organization serving children and families.

My name is Jean
and I am a fork… but not just any fork…
I am a **stainless steel** fork!

I'm very important because I help the people eat. The people use my sharp tines to lift their food up to their mouths. They also use me to hold their food while they cut it.

Because of me, the people don't have to use their fingers as much when they eat. So actually, I help the people have better table manners.

I just LOVE my job!

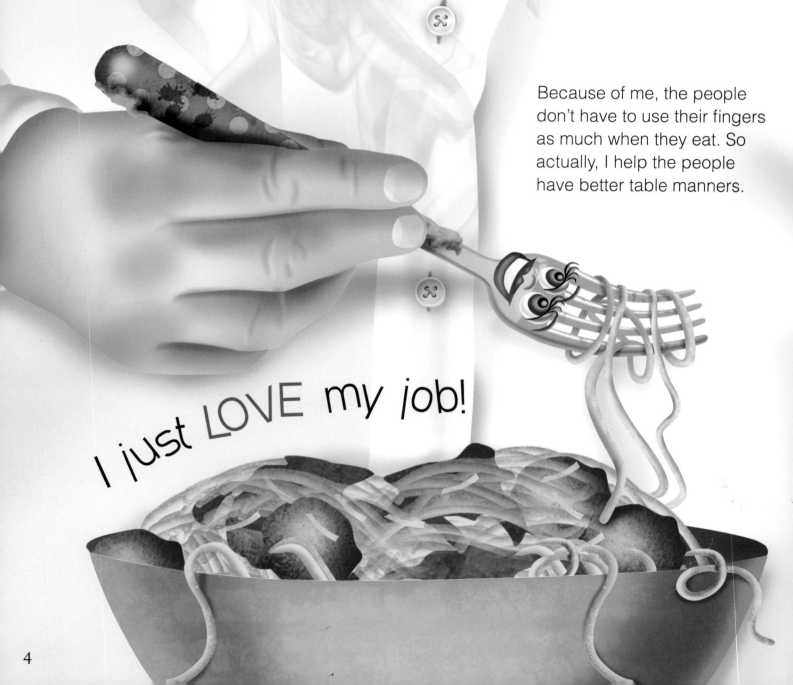

I like to hang out with the other forks, the knives and the spoons. They're my friends!

"Hi guys!"

"Hygiene...
you stink!"

"Hi guys! What's up?"

"Hygiene...
you stink!"

"Hey guys! Wanna hang out?"

"Hygiene...
you stink!"

Only sometimes, my friends
don't act like they want to
hang out with me.

5

"I just don't get it," I told Can Opener.

"The other silverware used to be pretty nice to me, and the people used to use me a lot. Now, I'm practically out of a job because I never get used by the people, and the other silverware won't have much to do with me either."

"Well, I hate to break it to you, my friend, Fork, but it appears you smell like last week's pork!

How long has it been since you've taken a bath, or a shower in the dishwasher? Just do the math."

$$\left(\begin{array}{c}\text{dirt} \\ \text{and} \\ \text{germs}\end{array}\right) + \left(\begin{array}{c}\text{soap} \\ \text{and} \\ \text{water}\end{array}\right) = \textbf{CLEAN}$$

You need to wash with soap every single day.
If you don't, your stinky smell will push your friends away."

"I don't think I smell that bad!"

"Fork, you're wrong!
I can smell you from here!
And you don't smell so sweet.
In fact, you **STINK**, my dear!"

"You are covered in bacteria
from your handle to your tines.
A little soap and *water*,
will help you really shine."

"I watched you yesterday
when the sink was full of bubbles.
All your friends just jumped right in.
But not you, you looked troubled.

Then you hid yourself under a napkin
so you wouldn't get tossed in the sink.
You didn't get washed and now you smell.
In fact, you really **STINK!**"

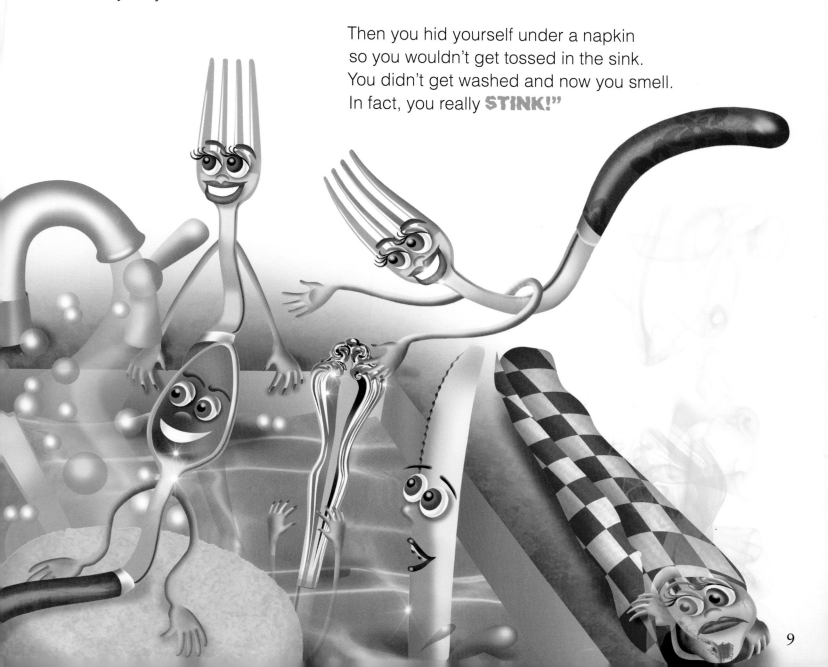

9

"But I don't like to take baths in the sink, or showers in the dishwasher!"

"Why?"

"I'm kinda afraid of the *water*.
And I might get **soap** in my eyes.
That happened once and it hurt so bad
that it even made me cry."

"Sometimes the water feels **TOO COLD**.
And sometimes it's way *too hot*.
And then I get water in my ears.
And I just LOVE that…

NOT!!!!!

Then when it's time for me to get out
I always feel really cold.
Besides, I'm made of stainless steel,
not iron, tin or gold."

11

"You have to use antibacterial soap,
toothpaste and shampoo,
to wash your stinky germs away
so your stainless can shine through."

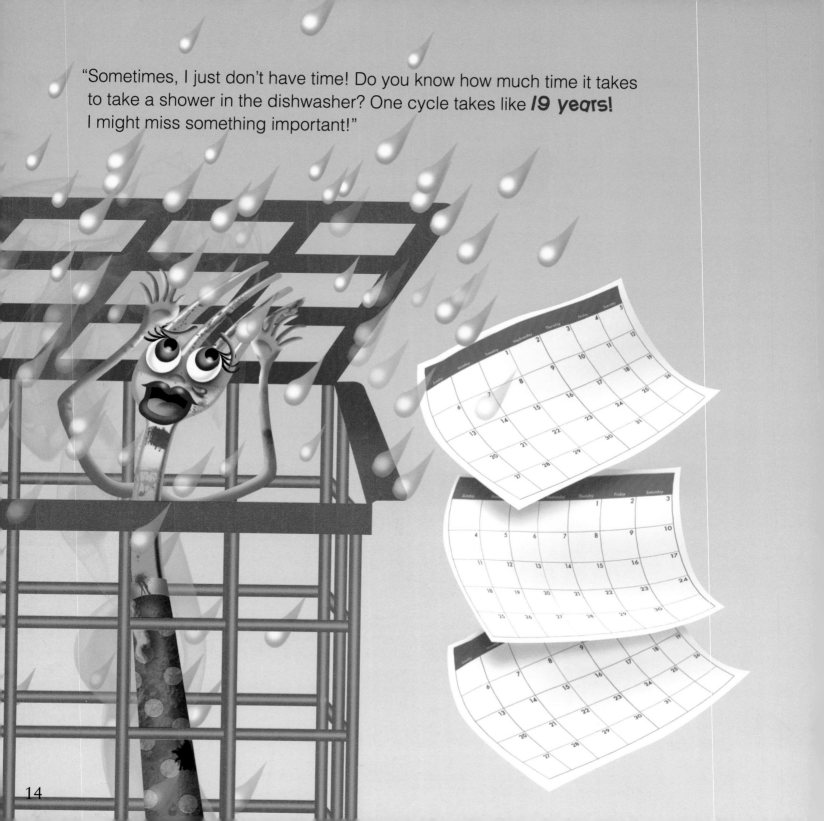

"Sometimes, I just don't have time! Do you know how much time it takes to take a shower in the dishwasher? One cycle takes like *19 years!* I might miss something important!"

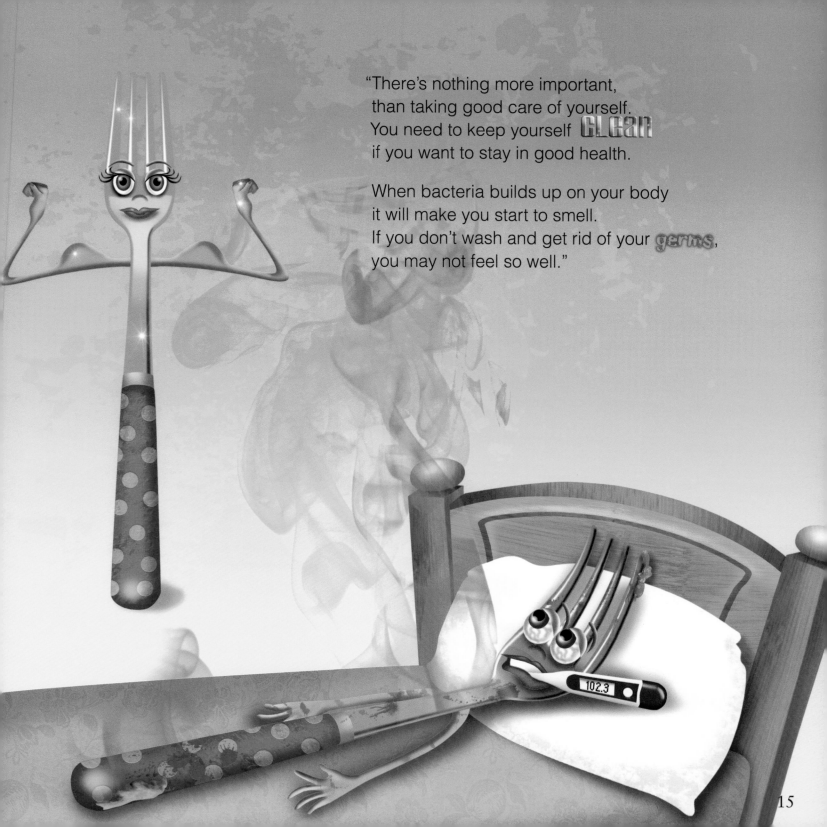

"There's nothing more important,
than taking good care of yourself.
You need to keep yourself CLEAN
if you want to stay in good health.

When bacteria builds up on your body
it will make you start to smell.
If you don't wash and get rid of your germs,
you may not feel so well."

15

"germs are NOT for sharing
and if you don't wash them off,
you might cause others to get sick.
They'll ache and sneeze and cough."

16

"No person wants to use a fork
that's not clean and free of germs.

They fear that you might make them sick,

or even
give them
WORMS!"

17

"Well… do I have to do it **every day?**"

"When you were a young fork, you didn't do as much,
and you could get away with skipping days.
But now that you're growing up, things are changing.
You get used more often, and you have a lot more
bacteria, so yes… you need to shower or bathe
every single day! There may even be days when
you have to take two baths or two showers, or
maybe one of each."

Sunday
Monday
Tuesday
Wednesday
Thursday
Friday
Saturday

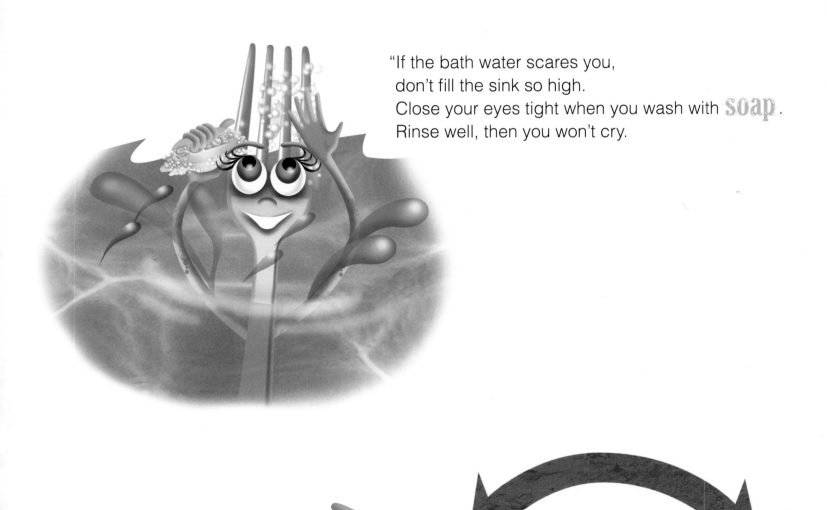

"If the bath water scares you,
don't fill the sink so high.
Close your eyes tight when you wash with soap.
Rinse well, then you won't cry.

If you get *water* in your ears,
tilt your head from side to side.
What goes in will always run out.
Start tilting, and give it a try."

"Make sure there's a clean dish towel close to you
so when you are finished cleaning,
you can dry yourself off quickly
and you won't get that

FRREEEEZZING
FEELING!

LA LA LA LA LA ...

If you get nervous showering in the dishwasher,
or it seems to take too long,
try out your voice and start singing
your very most favorite song."

21

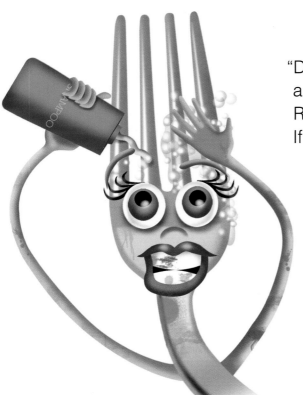

"Don't forget to wash your tines
and make sure you use shampoo.
Rinse your tines out really well.
If you don't they'll feel like glue.

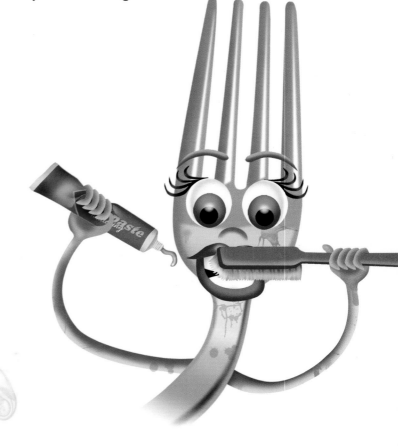

Also remember to brush your teeth
at least two times every day.
Your stainless steel might shine
    but if your breath still **stinks**,
your friends might push you away.

You are a stainless steel fork.
You have a very important job.
But if you don't keep yourself CLEAN,
you'll turn into a germy blob!"

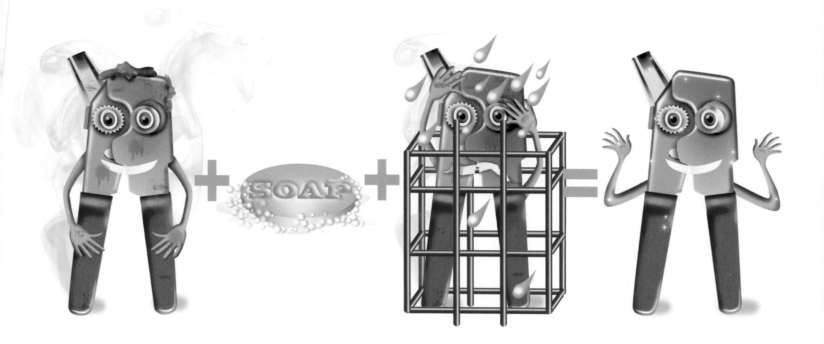

"You are a beautiful fork
and you're made out of stainless steel!
Trust me, Fork, believe what I say,
because I know just how you feel.

I used to have a problem with showers,
and I didn't like to take baths.
I started to stink, then I started to think…
and then I did the math."

$$\left(\begin{array}{c}dirt \\ and \\ germs\end{array}\right) + \left(\begin{array}{c}soap \\ and \\ water\end{array}\right) = CLEAN$$

"Now I get used by the people.
I get to open every can.
Everyone in the drawer loves me.
 And the spatula thinks I'm the MAN!"

$$\left(\frac{dirt}{germs}\right) + \left(\frac{soap}{water}\right) = CLEAN$$

"Brush your teeth, shampoo your tines
and wash all your parts with soap.
Do this every day
and your life will be filled with hope."

I'm Clean!

I thought about everything Can Opener told me, and I decided to give it a try.

"Hi Guys!"

"Hi Guys!"

"Hi, Jean… How's it **going?**"

"Hi Guys!"

"Hey, Jean…
You look **great!**"

"Hey, what's up?"

"Hey, Jean…
Let's hang **out!**"

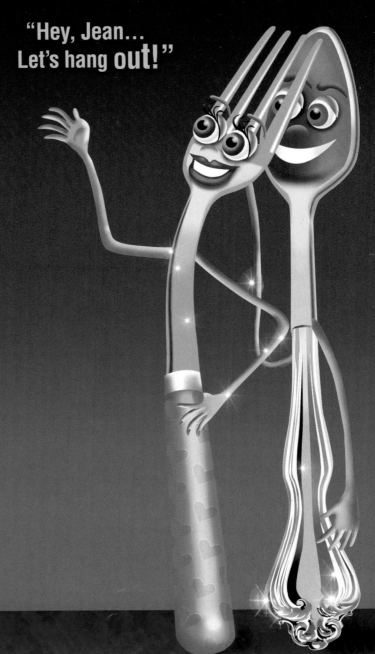

"I am a fork...
but not just any fork...
I am a clean, healthy, **stainless steel** fork..."

and I just LOVE my job!"

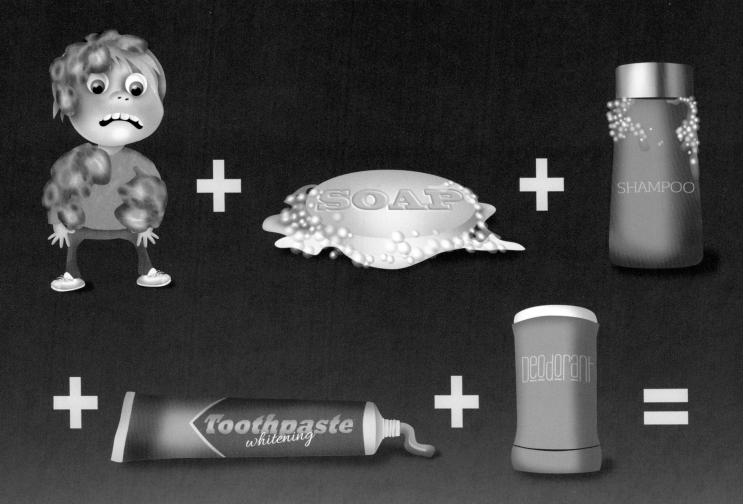

P.S

"If you are one of the people
and you just finished reading this book,
what I now do will help you, too,
improve the way you look.

But there is one thing that
you might need to add
when you are doing the math.

You may need to use deodorant
after showering or taking a bath."

(Seriously… should a fork use deodorant???? **NOT!)**

Tips for CLEAN Kids

PERSONAL HYGIENE can be a difficult subject to address and discuss with kids. Bodies sometimes mature faster than growing hygiene habits. It is very important to instill good hygiene practices early to prevent cavities, infections, numerous other health problems and social isolation.

There are many different ways to teach personal hygiene. Here are a few tips:

1. *(Dirt and Germs) + (Soap and Water) = CLEAN!* Explain the concept of germs and bacteria. A shower or a bath every day or two is a must. It is also very important to shower after participating in rigorous sporting events. Don't forget! Your hair is a part of your body and needs to be shampooed and thoroughly rinsed at least every other day.

2. Always use clean wash cloths and towels, and put on clean clothes after showering or taking a bath.

3. Teach the six steps of hand washing and discuss when and why hand washing is important. **Wet hands apply soap lather soap rub and scrub for 20 seconds rinse dry well.**

4. Create a dental hygiene plan that includes brushing at least twice a day, rinsing out your mouth after you eat, using dental floss and mouthwash. Discuss the detriments of gingivitis, cavities, and bad breath. Having an unhealthy mouth can cause pain, missed school, and even serious illness.

5. For older kids, use deodorant after showering or bathing, and every morning before getting dressed. Deodorant controls bacteria. The antiperspirant in deodorant limits sweating.

6. Gently wash your face one to two times each day with facial cleanser to prevent acne. Don't pick at acne. Picking your face will spread germs, cause inflammation, spread oil, and may cause scarring.

7. Clip your finger nails and toe nails often. Biting your nails exposes your mouth to many unwanted germs!

8. Practice shaving with kid friendly razors or popsicle sticks before using the real thing. Demonstrate how to effectively and safely shave faces, ankles, knees and underarms. Discuss the why, when and how of shaving.

9. *GIRLS:* Make up and other personal items such as hairbrushes should not be shared with others as they spread bacteria which can harm the body. Discuss feminine hygiene with your daughter early so she will know what to expect. Explain the different products, how to use them and how often to change them. Teach your daughter how to track her cycle so that she can be prepared.

10. *YOU are your child's hygiene instructor so* **be a good role model!**

parenting.org
from **BOYS TOWN**

Boys Town Press Books by Julia Cook

Kid-friendly books to teach social skills

COMMUNICATE with **Confidence**

A book series to help kids master the art of communicating.

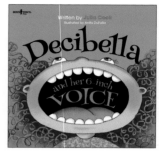
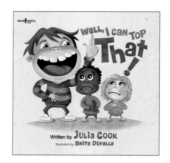

978-1-934490-57-0   978-1-934490-58-7

 **Building RELATIONSHIPS**   *A book series to help kids get along.*

978-1-934490-30-3   978-1-934490-39-6   978-1-934490-47-1   978-1-934490-48-8   978-1-934490-62-4

BEST ME I Can Be   *Reinforce the social skills RJ learns in each book by ordering its corresponding teacher's activity guide and skill posters.*

978-1-934490-20-4
978-1-934490-34-1 (SPANISH)
978-1-934490-23-5 (ACTIVITY GUIDE)

978-1-934490-25-9
978-1-934490-53-2 (SPANISH)
978-1-934490-27-3 (ACTIVITY GUIDE)

978-1-934490-28-0
978-1-934490-32-7 (ACTIVITY GUIDE)

978-1-934490-35-8
978-1-934490-37-2 (ACTIVITY GUIDE)

978-1-934490-43-3
978-1-934490-45-7 (ACTIVITY GUIDE)

978-1-934490-49-5
978-1-934490-51-8 (ACTIVITY GUIDE)

 **BOYS TOWN Press**

BoysTownPress.org

For information on Boys Town, its Education Model®, Common Sense Parenting®, and training programs:
boystowntraining.org | parenting.org
E-MAIL: training@BoysTown.org | PHONE: 1-800-545-5771

For parenting and educational books and other resources:
BoysTownPress.org
E-MAIL: btpress@BoysTown.org
PHONE: 1-800-282-6657